Pieces of
Christmas

$3.50 ★ POLAR POST ★

12 PM

CHRISTMAS DELIV...

DAILY

WORLD WIDE

Teri Sloat

Henry Holt and Company / New York

To Laura Godwin—
Thank you for letting me play

Henry Holt and Company, LLC
Publishers since 1866
115 West 18th Street
New York, New York 10011
www.henryholt.com

Henry Holt is a registered trademark
of Henry Holt and Company, LLC

Library of Congress Cataloging-in-Publication Data
Sloat, Teri.
Pieces of Christmas / Teri Sloat.
Summary: Short verses describe how animals around the world,
from yaks with yo-yos to The Nashville Newts, enjoy the special
gifts of Christmas that Santa Claus brings.
[1. Christmas—Fiction. 2. Animals—Fiction.
3. Santa Claus—Fiction. 4. Stories in rhyme.] I. Title.
PZ8.3.S63245 Pi 2002   [E]—dc21   2001005202

ISBN 0-8050-6355-2 / First Edition—2002
The artist used watercolor, Prismacolor pencil, acrylic, ink,
and graphite pencil to create the illustrations for this book.
Printed in the United States of America on acid-free paper. ∞
10 9 8 7 6 5 4 3 2 1

Kris Kringle comes on Christmas Eve
To visit us, if we believe.
No creature is too big or small,
Too young or old—he loves us all.

When Santa returns
    from making his rounds,
The letters he's answered
    lie drifted in mounds.
He calls the North Wind
    to blow them around,
And pieces of Christmas
    come swirling down.

Lizard dipped his tail in ink,
Said, "Just a minute, let me think . . ."
Then flipped his tail across the note—
MERRY CHRISTMAS! Lizard wrote.

"Around the World" and "Walk the Dog,"
Yaks yo-yo high above the fog,
With brightly spinning Christmas toys,
Filling mountaintops with joy.

Hear the tower bells? They're ringing.
Bats on belfry ropes are clinging,
Singing, swinging, to and fro,
Carols chiming as they go.

When the wind whistles carols through Africa,
The savanna grows peaceful at last,
And the lions lie watching in wonder
While wildebeests waltz through the grass.

Chameleons change from red to green
While skating for the king and queen,
Around the tree with lights that make
Them iridescent while they skate.

Christmastime means frequent stops
At crocodilian cookie shops,
For nothing brings out bigger smiles
Than cookies baked by crocodiles.

Raven called the birds together,
Asking each for one bright feather,
Flew off with these trees-to-go
To places where no trees could grow.

Come sail the Amazon with me,
Where toucans top the Christmas trees,
Like angels robed, with folded wings,
Trimmed in yellows, blues, and greens.

The smartest creature that I know
Is the sloth—he moves *s-o-o-o s-l-o-o-o-w*.
He's learned to make each Christmas last
Much longer by not moving fast.

On Pennsylvania Avenue,
Possums pray for me and you—
"Please bless this world, and bless this town,
And those whose lives are upside down."

Guided by the neon star
And music from the steel guitar,
The Nashville Newts have found their way
To play in Nashville Christmas Day.

*T*ravelers from the desert tell
Of dancing pigs and jingling bells,
And twinkling lights on cactus trees—
The Javelina Jamboree!

How bright the finch and cardinal,
The waxwing and the linnet.
Every tree's a Christmas tree
With winter birds perched in it.

The vole performed throughout the night.
He violined in black and white,
And people stopped to hear the sound
Of Christmas coming from the ground.

Spider walked across the sky,
Stringing stars as she walked by,
Then pulled her net to earth to light
The darkest places Christmas night.

"Come glide beside me," wrote the loon.
"We'll cross the lake upon the moon,
While stars go bobbing by our sides,
Come join me for a Christmas ride."

Santa sleeps 'neath a quilt
  and a blanket of down.
He dreams of a world
  that sleeps safe and sound
With a feeling of peace
  all the year round,
While pieces of Christmas
  cover the ground.